Amber's
First
Clue

The Mermaid S.O.S. series

Amber's First Clue

gillian shields

illustrated by helen turner

BLOOMSBURY

NEW YORK BERLIN LONDON

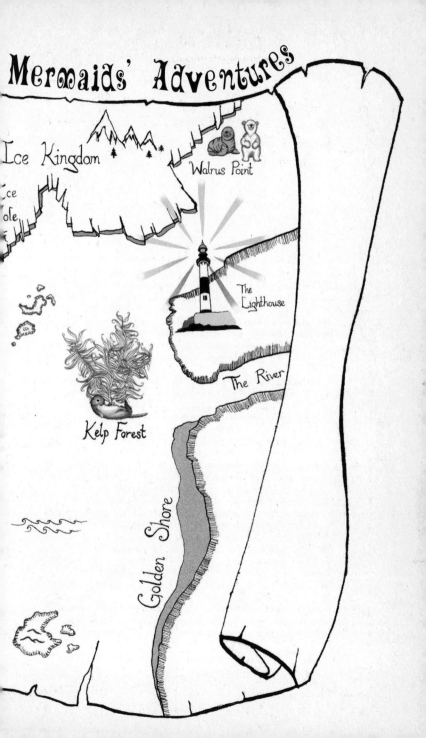

Originally published in Great Britain by Bloomsbury Publishing Plc. in 2007
First published in the United States of America in February 2009
by Bloomsbury Books for Young Readers
www.bloomsburykids.com

For information about permission to reproduce selections from this book, write to
Permissions, Bloomsbury BFYR, 175 Fifth Avenue, New York, New York 10010

Library of Congress Cataloging-in-Publication Data
Shields, Gillian.
Amber's first clue / by Gillian Shields ; illustrated by Helen Turner. — 1st U.S. ed.
    p.   cm. — (Mermaid S.O.S. series ; 2)
Summary: Amber leads her fellow mermaids in trying to help beluga whales that are
trapped in ice, while working on solving a riddle from evil Mantora, whose theft of the
snow diamonds may cause the Ice Kingdom to melt.
ISBN-13: 978-1-59990-336-1 • ISBN-10: 1-59990-336-9 (alk. paper)
[1. Mermaids—Fiction. 2. Adventure and adventurers—Fiction. 3. White whale—Fiction.
4. Whales—Fiction. 5. Narwhal—Fiction. 6. Ecology—Fiction.]
I. Turner, Helen. II. Title.
PZ7.S55478Amb 2009   [Fic]—dc22   2008032636

Printed in the U.S.A. by Worldcolor Fairfield, Pennsylvania
2 4 6 8 10 9 7 5 3

All papers used by Bloomsbury Publishing, Inc., are natural, recyclable products
made from wood grown in well-managed forests. The manufacturing processes
conform to the environmental regulations of the country of origin.

For Lily Rose

—G. S.

For my best friend, Laura

—Love H. T.

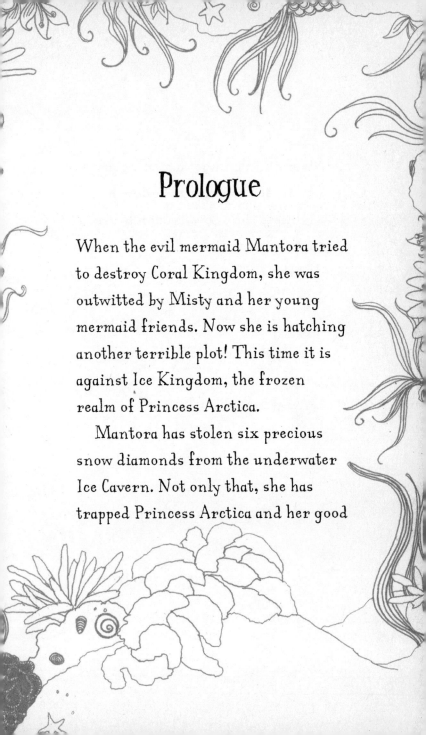

Prologue

When the evil mermaid Mantora tried to destroy Coral Kingdom, she was outwitted by Misty and her young mermaid friends. Now she is hatching another terrible plot! This time it is against Ice Kingdom, the frozen realm of Princess Arctica.

Mantora has stolen six precious snow diamonds from the underwater Ice Cavern. Not only that, she has trapped Princess Arctica and her good

Merfolk in a huge cage of enchanted icicles, so they cannot follow her.

Unless the snow diamonds are quickly returned to the Ice Cavern, the whole of Ice Kingdom will be destroyed and the distant southern lands will be flooded with melted ice.

Only Princess Arctica's courageous young mermaids—Amber, Katie, Megan, Jess, Becky, and Poppy—are small enough to slip through the jagged bars of Mantora's frosty cage. They are Sisters of the Sea, who are loyal to the Mermaid Pledge:

We promise that we'll take good care
Of all sea creatures everywhere.
We'll never hurt and never break,
We'll always give and never take.
And as we fight Mantora's threat,
This saying we must not forget:
"I'll help you and you'll help me,
For we are Sisters of the Sea!"

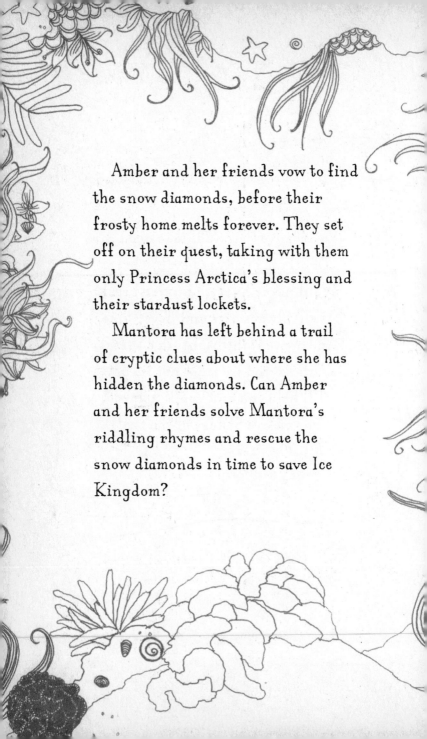

Amber and her friends vow to find the snow diamonds, before their frosty home melts forever. They set off on their quest, taking with them only Princess Arctica's blessing and their stardust lockets.

Mantora has left behind a trail of cryptic clues about where she has hidden the diamonds. Can Amber and her friends solve Mantora's riddling rhymes and rescue the snow diamonds in time to save Ice Kingdom?

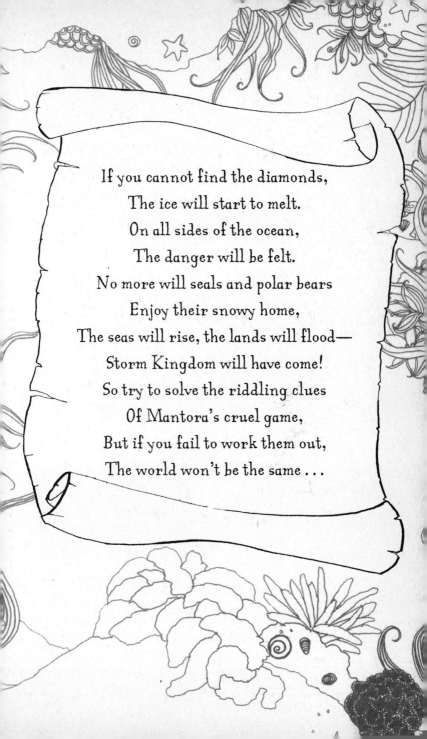

If you cannot find the diamonds,
The ice will start to melt.
On all sides of the ocean,
The danger will be felt.
No more will seals and polar bears
Enjoy their snowy home,
The seas will rise, the lands will flood—
Storm Kingdom will have come!
So try to solve the riddling clues
Of Mantora's cruel game,
But if you fail to work them out,
The world won't be the same . . .

Amber

Chapter One

"So this is the Ice Cavern," said Amber in an awed whisper. "I've never been here before."

She cautiously swished her sparkling lilac tail and swam into the middle of the underwater treasure store. Her young mermaid friends—Katie, Megan, Jess, Becky, and Poppy—followed her eagerly. They gazed up at the shining walls of ice that arched above them in a cluster of glistening icicles.

"It's so beautiful." Becky sighed, glancing around with wide eyes at the carved walls. They gleamed with frosty flickers of white and blue and turquoise.

It was the first time the young mermaids had seen the secret Ice Cavern, where the

snow diamonds were kept. The diamonds were full of magical power, which helped Mother Nature keep Ice Kingdom frozen.

"Wow," said Poppy as she swam slowly around the magical chamber. "Look at those!"

Amber and her friends stared in wonder at the six fabulous frozen statues that stood around the cavern. There was a darting fish, a flying bird, a glowing heart, a diving dolphin, a flowerlike anemone, and a shimmering star. The mermaids wove in and out of the statues, through the clear, cold water.

"Have you noticed that the statues are the same shapes as our new stardust lockets?" asked Amber, stretching out her arm gracefully. A silver bracelet shined on her wrist, and from the bracelet dangled a sparkling locket, carved in the shape of a leaping fish.

"You're right," agreed Jess. "Look, I've got the dolphin on my bracelet."

One by one, the mermaids raised their arms to admire their shining stardust lockets.

"My locket is in the shape of the seabird," said Katie. She examined her bracelet happily, then looked up at the matching ice carving.

"And mine is the anemone, which is like a flower in the sea," murmured Becky dreamily. "What is yours, Megan?"

"Oh, mine is the heart," said Megan, blushing.

"That must be because you're so kind."

Amber smiled. Megan was very caring to all the sea creatures, especially the tiny ones. She even had a pet shrimp called Sammy.

"Well, I've got the star," interrupted Poppy, with a bold grin. "So that must mean it's the best!"

"Don't be a show-off, Poppy," said Amber. "All the stardust lockets are beautiful, and they're all equally important. Remember, this isn't a game. Everyone in Ice Kingdom is relying on us."

The stardust lockets had been given to the young friends by Princess Arctica herself that very day—when disaster had struck Ice Kingdom!

The evil mermaid Mantora had sneaked into the kingdom and stolen the precious snow diamonds from the underwater Ice Cavern, which was hidden away below the Ice Palace. Clutching the diamonds in her greedy hands, Mantora had swooped into the palace itself. Then she had trapped Princess Arctica and her loyal Merfolk in an enchanted cage of gleaming black icicles.

Amber would never forget hearing Mantora's taunting words, echoing through the clear water.

"Now the snow diamonds are mine!"

Mantora had laughed scornfully. "If you want them back in time to stop Ice Kingdom from melting away, you will have to be very clever. I have left you a message, my dear Arctica, in your precious Ice Cavern. But first you must get out of this prison of icicles. That is the first puzzle that you must solve! Ha, ha, ha!"

With a swirl of her dark tail and cloak, Mantora had disappeared, her cruel laughter fading slowly as she swam away with the stolen treasure. The Merfolk didn't know what to do, but, luckily,

Amber and her young friends had been small enough to slip out of the enchanted cage with a wriggle of their bright tails.

"We'll go after her, Princess Arctica," Amber had promised, eagerly pushing her golden hair away from her face. "And we'll get the snow diamonds back somehow!"

"Wait, my brave young mermaids. Take my stardust lockets," Princess Arctica had urged them, unfastening her glittering jewels and passing them through the jagged bars of ice. "If you find the diamonds, keep them safe in these lockets until you can return them to the Ice Cavern. But you must work quickly, before Ice Kingdom begins to melt."

"Where should we look for the diamonds?" Jess had asked in a determined voice.

"Swim first to the Ice Cavern underneath the palace," the princess swiftly replied. "Mantora said she has left a message there. Perhaps it will be some kind of clue about how to get the diamonds back."

The good Merfolk who were trapped with Princess Arctica looked up with new hope at the courageous young Sisters of the Sea.

"But do you think we could really rescue the diamonds, Your Highness?" gulped gentle Megan. "We're only little mermaids. How can we fight Mantora?"

"Brave young hearts and minds like yours are what she fears the most," the princess had reassured her. "Also, the magical lockets I have given you are dusted with the light of the great North Star. They can guide and heal and help, in more ways than you can imagine."

27

The mermaids looked at their sparkling lockets in amazement.

"And even though I am now trapped by Mantora's spell," continued Princess Arctica, "I will somehow get news of our danger to my cousin, Queen Neptuna, in Coral Kingdom. She will do her best to send you help of some kind. Now go, and take the blessing of the Merfolk with you in this great task!"

Then the Merfolk had waved through the spiky icicle bars of their enchanted prison and called, "Good luck! Take care!" Blowing one last kiss to their families and summoning up all their courage, the mermaids had set off.

And so they had reached the secret Ice Cavern, hidden deep in the cool, turquoise waters. But as the friends were admiring the glittering ice statues and examining their lockets, Amber suddenly called out to them.

"Look!" she said, pointing dramatically to a solid pillar of ice in the middle of the cavern. On the top of the pillar was a carved silver casket, which glittered with a thousand tiny crystals. But the casket had been wrenched open, and it was now completely empty. The six snow diamonds, which had once nestled there safely,

29

really were gone! And the whole of Ice Kingdom was in grave danger without them.

Amber swam over to the broken casket, followed by her friends. They hovered together in the clear water around the pillar of ice.

"What's that at the bottom of the casket?" asked Becky, picking up a small scroll with her dainty fingers. It was made of dark green parchment and tied with bloodred strands of seaweed.

"It's a message of some kind," cried Katie. "Princess Arctica said we might find one."

"I don't like the look of it," said Megan as a shiver went down her spine.

"Read it to us quickly, Amber," added

Jess. "We need to know what it is, even if it's bad news."

Amber nervously undid the scroll and glanced at the cramped black letters. What would the strange message say?

Chapter Two

Amber took a deep breath and began to read aloud:

"Greetings to the mermaids who dare to read this message!
You must think you are very clever to escape my icicle cage, but trouble lies ahead for you. I am going to hide the snow diamonds where you will never find them.

The only way to get them back is to solve all
my rhyming riddles—but hurry up!
Ice Kingdom cannot survive without the
diamonds and their magical power.
This snowy realm will become too warm,
and its melted waters will flood far over the
southern lands.
All will be chaos and confusion.
Storm Kingdom will triumph!
So solve the clue to find the first diamond—
if you dare.
How I shall laugh, watching you struggle to
work it out ..."

"What does she mean?" puzzled Becky.
"Wait, there's something else," replied
Amber. "Listen!"

"Where you see white ghosts
By these snowy coasts,
There the diamond lies,
Away from prying eyes,
But you must dig deep,
Or else you will weep!"

"So that's her silly old clue." Poppy
shrugged. "It can't be that hard to solve."

Poppy wasn't frightened
of anything or anyone.

"It looks pretty hard
to me," worried Katie.
"What does she mean
by white ghosts? There
aren't any ghosts here!"

The mermaids
frowned as they tried to

34

work it out. Amber glided slowly around the Ice Cavern with her hands clasped behind her back, swishing her tail up and down. She glanced up at the glittering ice statues. They gave her an idea.

"The clue says that white ghosts are by the 'snowy coasts,' so they must be here in Ice Kingdom," Amber said thoughtfully. "These statues—and our stardust lockets— show all the different kinds of creatures in Ice Kingdom, who live under the light of the North Star and are loved by the Merfolk. Now, what are the white ghosts likely to be? Could they be fish? Or seabirds? Or something else?"

"Amber, that's so clever of you," said Megan admiringly. "Now, what kind of creature could possibly look like a ghost?"

They all stared at each other with puzzled expressions.

"Or *sound* like a ghost," replied Amber slowly.

"I think you're onto something, Amber," exclaimed Jess. "Mantora's riddle must be trying to trick us, so we have to think of something that isn't the obvious answer. What if she really means a creature that calls out in a sad sort of voice, something that just *sounds* like a ghost?"

The others looked around hopefully. Amber squinted with concentration.

"Owls!" she blurted out. "What about the snowy owls who fly over Ice Kingdom on the way to their homes in the northern lands? They sound sad and spooky sometimes."

"Amber, you've done it. You've solved the clue!" cried Katie and Becky.

"Not completely," objected Poppy, with a shake of her coppery curls. "We still don't know where the diamond is."

"But the first step is to try and talk to those owls," said Jess firmly. She flicked her strong turquoise tail and sped over to the secret entrance of the Ice Cavern. "Let's go up to the surface as quickly as we can to look for them!"

The others followed her, rippling their pearly tails through the icy water. Only Amber waited for a moment, taking one last look at the empty casket. She knew that Princess Arctica was relying on her and the other young mermaids to save the snow diamonds—and the whole of Ice Kingdom. It was Amber's first important task, and she was determined not to fail.

"When we come back, we'll bring the snow diamonds with us," she promised in a whisper, glancing around at the glittering statues. Then she swiftly darted after her friends.

Jess led the way from the Ice Cavern, swimming up through the clear, green water to the sparkling surface of the

overwater world. As they reached the surface, the mermaids saw the frozen lands of Ice Kingdom all around them. The craggy tips of icebergs gleamed white and blue in the sun. The cold, deep sea lapped against a shore made of thick, flat stretches of ice, strong enough for polar bears to walk over.

Amber quickly caught up with her friends and swam with them to the ice edge. With a clever twist of their

glistening tails, the mermaids pulled
themselves out of the water. Their tails
glinted pink, peach, lilac, turquoise,
lemon, and blue, as they sat gracefully on
the smooth, white snow.

"Could you please get out your harp,
Katie?" asked Amber. "Then you could try
calling the owls for us. Let's hope they're
not too far away."

Katie was very musical and never went
anywhere without her delicate little
mermaid harp. It hung over her shoulder on
a braided cord. The lively, friendly mermaid
could make all sorts of special melodies to
call the birds and creatures to her.

Quickly, Katie strummed the harp's
golden strings and played a haunting tune.
It sounded just like the snowy owls calling

to each other. Very soon, Amber and her
friends could see the owls themselves,
gliding over the snow toward them.

"Good job, Katie," whispered Amber.
"That was quick work."

The snowy owls landed by the mermaids
in a flurry of soft white wings.

"Your music has called us from the
heights of the clear air, Sisters of the Sea!"

said the leader, whose name was Orlando. "How can we help?"

Amber quickly explained about the missing snow diamonds and the first clue.

"So you see," she said, "we wondered whether *you* might be the 'white ghosts' that Mantora was talking about. We thought you might be able to give us some help in solving the riddle."

The owls ruffled their feathers and laughed gently in funny, hooting voices.

"Ha-hoo-ha!" Orlando chuckled. "We've never been called ghosts before. I can assure you-hoo, my dear mermaids, we are all alive and well! And we have not seen anything of Mantora or the snow diamonds. We cannot be the 'ghosts' you are looking for."

Amber groaned. She had been so sure that she had solved Mantora's puzzle.

"Oh dear." She sighed. "We'll have to think again."

Orlando looked around kindly at their disappointed faces.

"We will do-hoo our best to help," he hooted. "We know how important it is to get the diamonds safely back to the Ice Cavern."

"Can you think of anything unusual that you have seen as you have flown over Ice Kingdom?" Jess asked quickly.

The owls went into a little huddle, softly cooing to each other. Then Orlando hopped over to Amber, blinking in the sunshine.

"There is one thing we can tell you-hoo," he said in a low voice. "We've seen one of the hoo-hoo-humans!"

"Humans?" murmured the mermaids, all asking questions at once. "Where? Are there a lot of them? Are they dangerous?" The friends were worried, because Princess Arctica and their parents had warned them not to go near any humans.

"Dangerous?" Orlando turned his head thoughtfully. "I don't know about that. This one was only small, and it looked very young, like you. It was one of the humans living in these snowy lands, who-hoo call themselves the Inuit people. And it was do-hoo-ing something odd."

45

"What was it doing?" asked Becky nervously. "Was it hunting?"

Orlando gave another snuffly hoot. "No, it wasn't hunting," he replied. "In fact, it was very strange. The odd little creature was sitting all by itself on the ice, far from the rest of its kind. And it was sobbing, with water streaming down its cheeks like raindrops."

"You mean it was crying!" exclaimed Megan. "Oh, Amber, the poor little thing."

Amber and her friends looked at one another in surprise. This was very mysterious—a human crying all by itself in the snow! What did it mean?

Chapter Three

"Perhaps we should take a peek at this human?" wondered Amber. "Is it far, Orlando?"

"Just on the other side of this snowy bank that sticks out into the water," replied the milk-white owl. "You-hoo could swim around there and see if this human has anything to do with Mantora's clue-hoo."

"No way!" said Poppy. "My mom says

the humans spoil the sea and everything that Mother Nature made. I'm not going anywhere near a human and that's that!"

"You'll have to, if the rest of us think we should," said Jess hotly.

"Let's not fight," pleaded sensitive Becky. It made her sad to see her friends argue. "Amber, you're always so sensible. What do you think we should do?"

Amber looked worried. "I think we're going to have to do lots of strange new things while we're looking for the snow diamonds," she replied. "Let's start by taking a look at this human, to find out what is going on. Thank you, Orlando, and good-bye!"

The owls slowly flew away into the distance. Amber slipped from the snow

into the cold blue sea, with a ripple of her
lilac tail. Then she beckoned her friends
to follow her as she swam around the
gleaming white tip of the ice. When she
reached the other side, Amber glanced
cautiously toward the open stretch of wide,
smooth ice.

Huddled on the ice, sitting in a sad
heap a few feet from the water's edge, was

the human.

"But it's only a
little girl!" exclaimed
Amber softly to her
friends as she
bobbed up and down
in the waves. "She's
not much older than
we are."

49

"And she seems so unhappy," whispered tenderhearted Megan.

The little girl was hunched next to a round hole in the ice. She was looking away from the mermaids, but they could see that she wore a soft, thick coat and a snug fur collar to keep her warm. The girl had silky black hair, and her dark eyes were wet with tears.

"I'm going to try and talk to her," said Amber boldly. "Besides, it's only the grown-up humans we mermaids have to hide from. Princess Arctica once told me that the human children love the sea and its creatures almost as much as we do. I'm sure this girl will help us."

"Or more likely *we'll* have to help *her*," muttered Poppy under her breath.

Amber swam quickly over to the ice edge and Jess, Becky, Katie, and Megan darted along behind her. Poppy followed sulkily. Soon, all the mermaids had pulled

themselves expertly from the waves onto the flat, smooth ice.

"Excuse me," called Amber in a low voice. "What is your name?"

As Amber spoke to the human child, she heard her stardust locket tinkle softly, like an icy bell. The locket's magical powers allowed all creatures near it to understand each other's language. Then, the girl whipped around to see who was speaking to her.

"Merfolk!" she gasped, hurriedly wiping the tears from her eyes. "Can it really be true? I was wishing for something magical to happen, and it did!" She looked around excitedly at the mermaids, and her face glowed with delight. "My name is Ana, and I've always wanted to meet the Sisters of the Sea. My grandmother once told me that you live deep under the icy waters. But I can hardly believe that you're real!"

"I promise you that we are," replied Amber politely. "What were you wishing for?"

Ana's face fell again. All her joy at meeting the mermaids seemed to drain away.

"I was wishing for a miracle to help my friend Benjy," she said sadly. "These blocks of ice have moved on the tides of the sea and have trapped him on all sides. Benjy is

stuck in a little pocket of cold water under here." The unhappy girl gazed gloomily into the hole in the ice. "He comes up to this hole to breathe, but he is getting weaker every day."

"Is Benjy another . . . like you . . . I mean, is he a human?" stammered Becky shyly.

"No!" said Ana. "If he were one of the Inuit, my father would help him. But Benjy is a baby beluga, one of the small whales who live in the northern seas. My father says the movement of the ice, which has caught him and his kinsfolk, is Mother Nature's way

and we cannot interfere." She began to cry softly, hiding her face in her furry sleeve.

Amber looked at Ana with a concerned expression. "Is there anything we can do to help?" she asked gently.

"Oh no, I don't think there is," said Poppy quickly. "If you haven't forgotten, Amber, we're supposed to be on a very urgent mission. Don't forget that Princess Arctica is trapped as well. I think we should concentrate on rescuing her and the diamonds, instead of getting distracted by a human. And we've got more important things to worry about than one young beluga."

"Poppy!" said Megan. "That's not very nice."

"Well, it's true," said Poppy, turning

up her nose and tossing her bright curls
defiantly.

"Yes, it is true, in a way," replied
Amber, looking serious and thoughtful.
"We can't stop thinking about how to
solve the first clue. But our stardust lockets
tell us that all the creatures of Ice
Kingdom are important."

"And the heart on Megan's locket is
perhaps more important than anything,"
said Becky softly.

"Yes," agreed Amber. "Ana loves her
friend Benjy, and I think Princess Arctica
would want us to help. What do the rest of
you think?" She glanced at each of her
friends in turn.

"You're right, Amber," declared Jess.
"Anyway, we're stumped on the clue for

the moment. Maybe we'll get some inspiration while we're helping Benjy."

"Oh, will you really help?" breathed Ana, sitting up and brushing away her tears. "I'd be so grateful!"

"Of course we want to help," said Katie. "Agreed, Poppy?"

"Oh, all right, I suppose," muttered Poppy reluctantly. "Agreed."

"That's settled then," said Amber. "We all want to rescue Benjy. The question is—how?"

Chapter Four

At that moment, Ana's face lit up and she cried, "Look, Benjy is here!"

A smooth gray face poked shyly above the little hole in the ice. It was a baby beluga whale, who looked very hungry. Ana stroked his cheek and kissed his nose.

"Ana has asked us to help you and your family, Benjy," explained Amber.

"Thank you, Sisters of the Sea," said

Benjy faintly, looking up at the mermaids sitting on the frosty snow. "We are getting weak, stuck in this narrow pool and trapped by the ice."

"If Benjy and the other whales don't get out to their feeding grounds very soon, they will starve," added Ana, her eyes dark with worry.

"But what are we going to do, Amber?" whispered Jess urgently. "We can't just lift the whales out of the hole and drag them over the ice to the sea!"

"I'm not sure what to do yet," Amber confessed. "But this breathing hole is close to the ice edge, so the whales are trapped very near to the open sea. The wall of ice blocking them in can't be very thick. What if we found some way of cutting through it?"

"That's a good idea," said Megan. "Then the whales could swim through the opening we made and be free again."

"So what could we use to cut the ice?" wondered Becky.

"I've got something that might help," suggested Ana. "Look—my own little knife that my father carved for me." She proudly pulled a small, shining blade from a soft bag at her side.

"Thank you, Ana," said Amber gratefully. "We'll try that."

With a flick of their spangled

tails, the mermaids dived into the turquoise waves that lapped against the ice edge. Then they sank under the surface and looked around carefully. On one side of them, the deep, cold sea stretched away into the distance. On the other, a great wall of ice shone with glints of blue and purple and green.

"Benjy and the others must be stuck behind here," said practical-minded Jess. "The ice has trapped them on all sides—above, around, and below. Let's get to work to make them an escape tunnel!"

Amber and her friends took turns chipping away at the smooth cliff of ice with Ana's little knife. Glittering splinters broke off, but it was slow work. The mermaids' arms started to ache, and they still hadn't made much progress.

"This is useless," said Poppy impatiently. "It will take us forever to make a tunnel."

"Have you got any better ideas, Poppy?" asked Katie.

"Yes, I have actually," replied Poppy, with a confident flourish of her sparkly blue tail. "We need something much

bigger than this little baby knife. We need something huge, like a battering ram, which will smash this ice to pieces!"

"But we don't have anything like that," Amber protested.

Poppy suddenly twisted her tail and did a dazzling somersault in the water.

"That's where you're wrong, Amber." She laughed. "We do have something really huge. Look behind you!"

All the mermaids turned around and gasped. Gliding near them in the underwater depths was a large, mottled narwhal. The strange-looking creature was a special kind of whale, with a strong, straight tusk that stuck out from his head like a spear.

"His long tusk would be perfect for

breaking the ice," said Amber excitedly.
"Good eye, Poppy."

"I said it was a good idea, didn't I?"
replied Poppy with a grin.

Amber quickly swam over to the
narwhal to explain what was needed.

"Belugas trapped in the ice?" he said
in a gruff voice, solemnly wagging his
tusk up and down. "I don't mind stopping
for a moment. I'll soon smash a hole in
that ice. My tusk is the strongest in the

whole of Ice Kingdom, or my name isn't Magnus!"

"But you will be careful not to hurt the whales trapped behind the wall of ice, won't you?" asked Megan anxiously.

"Of course, of course," replied Magnus. "Just watch me!"

Magnus squared up to the sheer wall of ice and charged toward it with a surge of his powerful tail. CRASH! His tusk rammed straight into the ice, leaving a long, deep crack.

"That's it!" shouted the mermaids. "You're doing it, Magnus!"

Again and again, the powerful narwhal pounded against the wall of ice with his tusk, grunting with the effort. At last, a narrow tunnel began to open up, reaching almost all the way to where Benjy and his family were imprisoned. Strange, mournful noises echoed eerily down the tunnel.

"What's that spooky sound?" asked Katie, looking around and shivering.

"It's the beluga whales calling to each other, on the other side of this ice," puffed Magnus. "They can hear us, and they know we are trying to rescue them."

"And now there's only a thin block of ice separating us from the whales," said Amber hopefully. "If you charge it with your tusk one last time, Magnus, I think the whales will be able to swim out into the tunnel."

The mermaids put their hands on Magnus's broad shoulders to give him an extra push.

"One, two, three—*Mermaid S.O.S.!*"

they cried, and with one huge heave the last chunk of ice cracked into a thousand shattered pieces.

"Oh, thank you, Magnus," said Amber as they all wriggled out of the tunnel to make way for the beluga whales.

"Anytime you want something shifted, just call for Magnus," said the narwhal, waggling his tusk one last time. "My folk will always be happy to help the Sisters of the Sea. Good-bye!"

The mermaids waved gratefully to Magnus as he glided away. Then they waited anxiously for the whales to swim down the icy tunnel to freedom. First came Ana's friend Benjy, shining silver-gray in the water.

"And here are my mom and dad and aunts and uncles," he cried weakly. "You have rescued my whole family!"

Slowly, the thin and tired adult whales began to head out of their prison. But as they did so, the young mermaids got an unexpected surprise. The smooth skin of the fully grown beluga whales wasn't gray like Benjy's. Instead, it gleamed like pure, pearly-white snow.

As the white whales floated slowly out of the tunnel making their haunting cries, the young mermaids turned to each other and exclaimed, "The 'white ghosts'! We've found them!"

Chapter Five

Amber and her friends swam through the cold, clear water after Benjy, the baby whale. He was bravely making his way to the overwater world, where Ana was waiting for him at the ice edge. The little girl greeted Benjy with delight, then looked at the mermaids bobbing up and down in the sparkling waves.

"You have saved his life," Ana said gratefully.

"Not only that," replied Jess. "We've found the meaning of the first clue!"

"You see, Ana," explained Amber, "we need to save even more than your friend Benjy. An evil mermaid, Mantora, has stolen the snow diamonds that keep everything cool and frosty. If we don't get them back soon, Ice Kingdom will melt."

"That would be terrible," cried Ana. "If everything warms up, our home will be destroyed, and the whole world will be changed forever!"

All the mermaids shuddered. It was too horrible to imagine.

"Our only hope of finding the snow diamonds is to solve Mantora's fiendish clues," said Katie. "She thinks it's fun to taunt us with hints about where the diamonds really are."

"Mantora thinks we can't find them, but we're going to prove her wrong," added Poppy with a stubborn tilt of her chin.

"And now we're sure that the white ghosts in the clue are the beluga whales," said Becky, gently swirling her peach-colored tail in the water. "So we need to ask Benjy and his family if they have seen the diamond."

The graceful white whales slowly circled the young friends in the fresh, cool waves, enjoying their new freedom.

"Ask us anything you want, mermaids," they called in their echoing voices. "We want to repay you for rescuing us."

"Have you seen Mantora?" Jess asked eagerly.

"We haven't seen her," piped Benjy, "but we've heard her!"

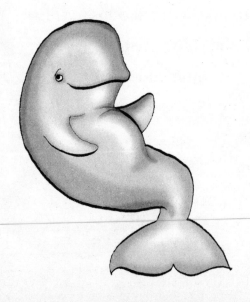

"What do you mean, Benjy?" said Amber, turning to the friendly baby whale with a smile. "Please tell us everything you heard."

"It was just before Ana came to see me today at the ice hole," said Benjy. "We were all swimming sadly in our little prison under the ice. Then we heard a strange sound above us. It came from the overwater world. But it wasn't Ana's gentle voice—it was horrible, sneering laughter. Then I heard someone boasting about 'Mantora's riddling rhymes' . . ."

"That was Mantora all right! What happened next?" urged Poppy.

"Something dropped into the ice hole," Benjy continued. "I thought it might be food, but it was like a sharp stone. It grazed my cheek—look! Then it sank to the bottom of the cave and slipped down a crack in the ice." Benjy's mother and father and the other belugas murmured in agreement.

"That sharp stone must have been the snow diamond," said Amber hurriedly.

"And don't you remember that the clue said something about 'digging deep'?" added Becky. "The diamond must be hidden deep at the bottom of that crack."

"Come on, everyone, back through the tunnel into the cave," cried Poppy. "I bet I'll see the diamond first!"

Amber dived back under the waves with a flash of her shining lilac tail. The others leaped after her like a bright rainbow. Now they really did have a chance of finding the first diamond! The mermaids' hearts were beating wildly with hope and excitement. They streamed down the underwater tunnel and into the icy cave, where the belugas had been trapped.

"There are cracks in the floor if you search closely," said Katie, looking through the water at the frozen layers beneath them. "But which one contains the diamond?"

Amber darted down toward a shadowy nook in a dark corner of the cave.

"I thought I saw something

75

twinkling down here!" she declared. The others gathered next to her, as Amber tried to peer into a deep, jagged crack in the ice.

"It's too dark," she said. "I can't see anything. We need a light . . . oh!"

She lifted up her wrist and stared at her bracelet in astonishment. Her silvery stardust locket, which was in the shape of a graceful fish, had started to glow.

"Look!" Megan

said. "All our stardust lockets are glowing, just when we needed some light to help us. Princess Arctica said they had magical powers, and she was right!"

The mermaids gratefully held their lockets up like gleaming lanterns, as rays of golden light poured out around them.

"I can see much better now, thanks to our stardust lockets," said Amber, peering down the deep crack. "Wait, there really *is* something sparkly down there . . . or is it just a splinter of glittery ice?"

The others hovered over the crack and tried to take a look as well.

"If only your locket could shine a little bit brighter, Amber," they murmured.

At that moment, Amber's stardust locket twirled around on her bracelet, shooting out bright silver sparks that lit up the deep crack like a firework.

"That's amazing!" cried Amber. "Now I can see all the way to the bottom of the crack. And I can see the diamond!"

Chapter Six

The mermaids hugged each other tightly.
They had solved the clue and found the
first snow diamond. All they had to do
now was put it away safely in Amber's
stardust locket.

"Oh, pick it up, Amber," urged her
friends.

Amber tried to slip her arm into the
crack in the ice. But the jagged opening

was too narrow for her to reach down
all the way to where the diamond was
lodged.

"I can't get to it," she gasped in dismay.
"Becky, you have smaller hands—can you
reach it?"

But even Becky's dainty fingers couldn't
grasp the tantalizing snow diamond.

"Let's just ask Magnus to come and
smash this ice with his tusk," suggested
Jess. "Then we'll reach the diamond
easily."

"No!" Katie interrupted with a shake of
her dark, glossy braid. "If Magnus breaks
the ice around the crack, the diamond
might fall into the deep sea below. Then
we would never find it again."

"Katie's right," said Amber, looking

around at her friends. "We need someone
with the tiniest fingers to reach into the
crack and lift the snow diamond out very
carefully. We are the smallest of the
Merfolk, but we're just too big."

She peered anxiously into the rough slit
in the ice once again. It was so tormenting
to be able to see the precious diamond but
not be able to reach it. Was this just
another of Mantora's cruel tricks? But Jess

suddenly let out a shout that echoed around the frozen cave.

"Well, if we mermaids can't reach it, what about a mermaid's pet?" she said, grinning. "Megan, is Sammy awake?"

Megan looked startled but then began to smile. "Of course!" she said. "Sammy is just the right size."

She gently reached inside the pocket of
her warm fluffy jacket, where Sammy was
snoozing. He was a teeny creature called a
fairy shrimp. They usually lived in shallow
pools at the edge of Ice Kingdom's snowy
lands, but Sammy went everywhere with
Megan, snugly tucked into a deep corner
of her pocket.

He woke up and sat on Megan's hand,
peering around sleepily. Megan stroked his
head tenderly and explained about the
diamond. As she did so, a stray sprinkle of
stardust from Megan's locket landed on
her beloved pet. Sammy waved his feathery
feelers eagerly. For a moment, he was
surrounded by tiny shooting stars.

"I feel different," he panted. "I feel brave
and strong and *magical*!"

Then he leaped off Megan's hand and quickly disappeared down the deep crack in the ice. For a few moments Amber and her friends held their breath. Would Sammy be able to lift the heavy diamond? But before they had time to fret, the brave little shrimp was back again, huffing and panting but clutching the precious jewel. The stardust sprinkle had given him extra special powers.

"Here you are," Sammy squeaked, tipping the heavy diamond into Amber's hand. It burned white like a star and yet shimmered with a hundred sparkling colors.

"We've found it," cried the friends. "Great job, Amber! And good work, Sammy!"

"Don't forget that our new friends Ana

and Benjy helped us, too," Amber reminded them gently. "We had to follow our hearts to find what we really wanted."

Poppy blushed for a moment. "I'm sorry I was mean about them earlier," she said, all in a rush. "I know, let's go and show them the diamond. I'm sure they'll want to see it."

Soon Amber and the other mermaids were cuddled up next to Ana on the edge of the ice. Benjy and his family swam in the deep blue water just near them.

"This is the first snow diamond, Ana," said the mermaids. "We couldn't have found it without you."

Ana looked very pleased as she held the glimmering jewel in her little gloved hand. "It's so gorgeous," she said, her eyes lighting up with wonder. "How could anyone be selfish enough to steal it?"

"Mantora is totally selfish," replied Amber. "She wants to destroy Ice Kingdom and spoil everything that Mother Nature made."

"Ugh!" Ana shivered. "She sounds horrible. I didn't know there were any mermaids like that."

"There aren't many, thank goodness," Megan reassured her. "My mother told me that Mantora turned bad because she was so jealous of her sister, the great Queen Neptuna."

"That's such a pretty name," said Ana, carefully giving the diamond back to Amber. "Who is she?"

"There are lots of different kingdoms of the Merfolk," Katie explained. "In Ice Kingdom we are ruled and protected by our very own Princess Arctica. But Queen Neptuna in Coral Kingdom is the wisest mermaid of them all."

"Coral Kingdom!" repeated Ana with shining eyes. "I wish I could go there."

"So do I," agreed Becky, looking dreamily toward the faraway south. "I've heard it's one of the most beautiful places in the world. There are colorful corals, and all sorts of amazing fish, and turtles and dolphins, and delicious warm seas . . ."

". . . our sea in Ice Kingdom will soon be

much too warm for us, if we don't find the other diamonds," Jess cut in, with a brisk nod of her dark curls. "Let's keep looking for them!"

"Jess is right," said Amber to the others. "This is only the start of our quest. We can't rest until we have found all six diamonds. And we don't know where our search will take us next."

"I wish I could help you." Ana sighed. "It would be a way of thanking you for saving Benjy's life. But my family will be expecting me at home. I must go now."

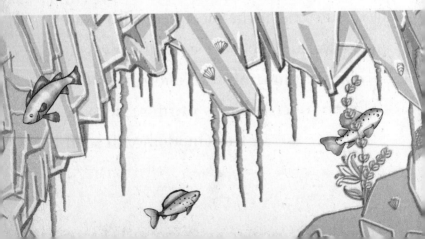

She stood up and brushed the snow from her furry leggings. "Benjy and I will be waiting for you when you get back with the six snow diamonds," she added. "Here, take my little bag. It contains some things you might need for your task."

"Thank you, thank you," cried the mermaids, waving at their young friend as she trotted away happily across the glinting snow. "Good-bye, Ana!"

"You see, Poppy, some humans can be good and kind," said Megan quietly. "I'm glad we have Ana as our friend."

"So am I," replied Poppy with a grin.

"Why don't you put the diamond away in your locket, Amber?" suggested Katie. "Then we can decide what to do next."

Amber opened her delicate locket and

gently dropped the shimmering diamond inside it. But then she noticed something.

"Look!" she said. "There's a long, silky thread tied around the diamond. It must be attached to something at the other end."

Carefully pulling on the thread, Amber reeled it toward her like a fisherman trying to land a plump trout. But on the very end of the delicate thread was the strangest thing.

"It's another scroll," gasped Becky.

"This must be a message from Mantora," said Amber. "I wonder what it says."

The mermaids crowded around Amber to look at the sinister twist of purple parchment.

"It's got to be another clue," said Poppy.

"Well, we solved the first one, didn't we? Let's see if we can outwit Mantora again."

The second clue! What would it say? And would the young mermaids be able to figure it out in time to find the second snow diamond?

Amber was so glad that she had successfully followed the first clue, and that the first diamond was safe in her stardust locket. But as she held the mysterious scroll in her hands, Amber knew that the adventures were just beginning for the Sisters of the Sea . . .

Amber has golden curls and a gleaming lilac tail. She looks after her friends and is a good leader.

Katie enjoys playing her mermaid harp. She has a long braid over her shoulder and a sparkly lemon-colored tail.

Megan has sweet wavy hair and a spangled pink and white tail. She is never far from her pet fairy shrimp, Sammy.

Jess is bold and brave, with dark curls and a dazzling turquoise tail. She is friends with Monty, the humpback whale.

Becky loves the beauty of the sea. Her hair is decorated with flowers, and her tail is a pretty peach color.

Poppy has coppery curls, a bright blue tail, and loads of confidence, but her impatience can land her in trouble.

Read all the books in the Mermaid S.O.S. series!